'Til 100

Ora Schiller

1

Dedicated to Karuna and Mom

Prologue

I look up at the blank ceiling, wishing a nurse or doctor would come check in. I can't believe I'm thinking that, but it's true. I haven't seen a doctor or nurse forever. I want to get out of bed, but I can't. Someone has to come at some point, won't they? "Mom it's you! I have never been so happy to see you!" I yell as the words echo around the room.

"That's strange," she says. "But you have a test soon about why you keep passing out." I already know why and I know they won't ever find out unless I tell them. But I won't tell them, not ever. This is what it's really like, my life in the hospital.

Chapter 1

The Track

"Hun are you ready?"

"No." I started the track. The track is when I count non stop but I only count 'til 100, but don't breath at all. I don't want them to think something is really wrong with me, but they can't know, at least not yet. For the past few years, I have been in the hospital. All the nurses are nice- well kind of. "Hi Doctor Sam," I say.

"Hello Lily. What are you doing? It looks like you have a test in a minute," Doctor Sam says.

"I'm going to the test room," I say, smirking.

"The test room is the other way," he says with a frown on his face.

"Well...I'm going to the bathroom," I say, pretending I'm looking at something. "What are *you* doing?" I ask him. His sweet voice turns icy cold.

"Go to the bathroom nearest to the test room," he says with a glum face.

"Bu..." I say.

"Go" he says, interrupting me.

"Okay, but the donut stand has rainbow sprinkles," I say sadly.

"No," he says and strides off. I wheel to the stand so quickly I almost fly out of my wheelchair. Of course I get rainbow sprinkles. After that I wheel to the test room and in only two minutes I hear the numbers again pounding, 67, 68, 69...100. They see that whatever has been happening is happening again. I can't stop, 98, 99, 100. I start to stop, but I pick it up again and pass out on the spot. Then about 3 hours later I hear muffled voices. Some of them are probably the doctors trying to see what just happened and some are probably my family. A small pounding comes back 5, 6, 7, 8, 9... 89...100, but this time the numbers turn into memories, memories only one person knows about.

Chapter 2

Finding The Memory

I wake up to find my mom rummaging around in her suitcase. "Mom, what are you doing?" I say.

"Oh nothing, just a bit of... a bit of... nothing," my mom says. I glare at her. After she leaves I start hearing the pounding again. 87, 88, 89...99, 100. The same thing happens. They turn into memories, memories I don't even remember. I can't tell whose faces they are or where they are, but I had to have been there. How else would I remember them? I get startled by the doctors trying not to spook me, though they do. They know something is really wrong. Dr. Sam comes in with a vial of blood. I know exactly what my mom was looking for. I had wondered why my mom took my blood from the old hospital, but now I know.

"Lily, is something wrong?" He asks. I look up at him, not knowing if I should tell him the truth.

"No," I say. He looks at me not knowing whether I am telling the truth or lying. All the doctors leave my room. I try to remember what was going on in the memory, but then I hear it: 45, 46, 47, 48...98, 99, 100. The memory still doesn't look familiar. All I see is smoke and a girl at the side of the road. I hear the sound of a... a... I can't remember. Just then my mom comes in.

I would have rather gotten a donut and eaten it while watching something on TV, but mom insists on going for a walk. More of a "wheel" to me. I accidentally say it out loud, "More of a wheel to me." My mom glares at me.

"Hun, it will be fun. You'll get to see everything," she says happily.

"Yeah, everything that includes cars and buildings," I mutter under my breath. I can't tell if my mom hears it, but… I… I… my mom looks at me worried, then I start: 88, 89… 98, 99, 100. The memories start again. This time I recognize some of them. At least I think I do. I remember being in a car, driving somewhere. I can't tell the details. I know I was with somebody, but who? I recognize the girl on the road, but where have I seen her before? Then I hear a voice.

"Just count 'til 100," the girl says. The words "one hundred" echo in my mind. I wake up. I look up at my mom, not even noticing that I'm awake yet. She was just covering her eyes, looking away.

"Mom, was I ever in a car crash?"

"What? Of course not, my darling." I don't know if my mom is lying or not. Maybe it wasn't me. Maybe I was watching it. But it feels like I was there. It feels like... like... I was *in* the car. But then, it hits me. I remember. At least I think I do. Was I with the girl on the road? The girl who said "count 'til 100"? I get sucked into the memory one more time. But this time, it has all the details.

Chapter 3

What Really Happened
Or did it?

Ava and I jumped in the car. We were going to see a movie. We were in 5th grade. Our parents would meet us there, but we wanted the feeling of being in an Uber. It was Ava's idea to do it in the first place, but I wasn't sure about it. Ava said, "It will be fine, and then we'll get to see the movie." Ava looked at me with her sparkly blue eyes. We set off. Ava and I were just talking the whole time, then we all saw smoke coming from the side of the road. I'm pretty sure somebody had a car accident, but then I saw our driver's head droop over the side of the seat. Ava wasn't looking at the driver. I didn't know where she was looking.

"Ava," I said.

She looked at me and said, "Just count 'til one hundred, you'll be fine." But then we crashed. First thing, the door swung open. Then I saw Ava on the side of the road, scratched and bruised. Then I bonked my head on the side of the door. It pushed it open, I fell out and my legs got caught under the wheel. The last thing I saw was Ava and the last words she said were, "'til one hundred."

Chapter 4

My Infection

My infection started out as a simple bruise. Then a tiny infection, but then it got so bad that I had to be in a wheelchair. And my concussion got so bad that I couldn't remember what caused it. At the time, I didn't know why people kept talking about Ava. Who was Ava anyway? My memory got so bad, I now can't ever leave the hospital, at least not anytime soon. The doctors don't know what is making my legs not be able to even move a single toe. They can't just keep me in bed forever and wait until I can move my legs. I have to get a test to see if I will ever be able to walk again, but the results are not good. My legs either have to be in a wheelchair or get a surgery to amputate my legs and put on prosthetic legs.

Chapter 5

Shocking News

I wake up on a Saturday morning, looking around to see if anyone is in my room. Then the track starts. 46, 47, 48... 98, 99, 100. This time I'm confused about why I am counting. The memories still come back to me, only clips of them. I look over to the window and for some weird reason basically all the doctors and nurses are outside. Right as some of the doctors turn around, I close the shades to the window. I can faintly hear what they are saying. Something about... about... 46, 47, 48... 85, 86... 96, 97, 98, 99, 100. Then my mom comes in. She has a startled look on her face. I bet my mom is about to tell me what everyone is talking about. Surprisingly she just says "Oh hun, you're getting so much better every day" and sits down without another word. That's strange. My mom helps me to get in my wheelchair and I wheel to the lounge (the lounge is a place where patients rest) only two doctors come in. The first one doesn't even notice I'm there and then leaves. But then Doctor Sam comes in and when I ask about what they were doing outside he doesn't hesitate. His eyes don't break out in tears like my mom would have, but instead he says it very slowly and calmly.

He says, "The hospital may have found a cure for your legs, but there is a 50% chance it could kill you." my face turns pink. I wheel away before Doctor Sam can ask me another question. Today I found shocking news.

Chapter 6
Trying Too Hard

I would have told my mom that I already know, but I don't want her breaking out in tears even more. On Saturday I usually have a test, but today they say, "You don't have to take the test any more." But to me that means more than not having to feel all the doctors poking around. To me this means I am becoming a normal girl.

Since I have an hour off I go to the donut stand, get a fudge and sprinkled donut, then I go back to my room and watch *Jumanji*. An hour passes and I pause the movie to go to a group my mom signed me up for. I go in the room and to my surprise it isn't a therapist, it's a group of people who need to talk. I go over to everyone, but one girl is sitting in what looks like a fuzzy pink droplit. I'm scared I'm going to start counting again.

I look around and then hear a man say, "Hello everyone. I would like you to say your name and why you're in the hospital. Does anyone want to start? No one, okay then I will start. My name is Mark and I am in the hospital because I work here." He points to me.

"Oh me? Well my name is Lily and I am in the hospital because... because..." I hear the loud pounding come in my head. 1,2,3,4,5,6,7,8...89... 98, 99, 100. I see the memory one more time and this time I see someone else. She isn't Ava or me, it's another girl. Could the memory that I saw have one missing part? Then I notice that everyone is watching me. I feel so embarrassed.

"Well we know why you are in the hospital," Mark says. A girl sitting across from me looks at me hopefully. After the class she walks over to me.

"Hi, um I was wondering if… never mind." The girl looks desperately at me then walks away, but first she mutters something under her breath. Then she turns around and asks, "What's your name?"

"Lily, what's yours?" I say.

"Claire," she says and walks away.

I wheel away, "MOM!!" I scream. "WHY DID YOU SIGN ME UP FOR THAT SUPPORT GROUP ANYWAY?"

"Oh hun I just thought you should talk to them."
She says with a sweet face. I go to the donut stand
and am in the lobby when I see Doctor Sam.

He looks at me and says, "Ever since I told you
about the cure you have been trying too hard."
He walks away. He wasn't wrong. I was trying a
little too hard to be normal, but he had told me
something I don't think I was ready to hear.

Chapter 7

My Decision

The next day, I wake up and see my dad sitting in a chair beside me. "Dad," I whisper. "What are you doing here?" My dad doesn't really come to the hospital to visit me a lot because he lives so far away, so I'm surprised to see him now. He only comes about once a month and he already visited two times this month.

"Oh Lily, I just wanted to be here for you. I'm never around and I thought It could help you make your decision and... and who knows what you'll pick." He says in a whisper. I look around my room and see something taped to the wall.

Something big, almost like a chart. I can vaguely see the words on the top. It reads, "Lily Stevens Medical Care."

"Dad, what's that on the wall?" I ask. He stands up and walks over. He reads aloud, "Lily Stevens Medical Care."

> Lily Stevens you have two weeks to decide which choice you will make. We will remind you what those choices are.
>
> 1: You could get surgery to amputate your legs and get prosthetic legs.
> 2: There is a cure, there's a 50% chance you may not survive and a 50% chance you could be cured forever.
> 3: You could choose to live the rest of your life in a wheelchair.

You need to tell a parent or doctor your decision. If you do not decide in two weeks your parents will have to decide for you.

- Dr. Sam

My dad looks puzzled. "Dad," I say. "Are you okay?" My dad looks at me then blinks and turns around.

"I'm fine hun." He says and walks over to the sink to get some water. He drinks 2 cups of water before he falls in the armchair beside my bed.

"Dad, thanks for coming. I am happy you respect my decision." I say in a soft whisper.

He looks at me and says, "I think I am going to check in with your mother. Is that all right?"

"Yes," I say.   He gets up and leaves without another word. I feel the wind blow from the open window next to my bed. I close it. I feel like I just arrived at the hospital, wishing a nurse or doctor would check in.

Then Doctor Sam comes in and says, "Lily you look dreadful, are you ok?" I don't answer. "Lily?!" He says in a strong voice.

"I am fine" I lie.

"Ok, did you see the notice? The one on your wall?" He asks.

"No" I lie again.

"Well here, read it." He says, handing the chart to me. Then he leaves. I look up at the blank ceiling, trying to concentrate on what the chart says.

Three choices, two weeks, could die.

It makes me think harder on what I choose. I'm still new to all of it. I press the button that will send a doctor coming. Doctor Greenberg, a tall woman, comes in, helps me into my wheelchair, and I set off. I search all the halls until I find the office. To my delight, it's Mark (the person who did support group) who says hello to me first. "Hi Mark, um… um do you remember Claire from the support group?" I ask.

"Of course I remember Claire. She was the one who kept looking at you." He says, looking cheerful.

"Oh that's weird, but anyway do you know what her room number is?" I ask.

"Hmmmmmm, oh yes room 214," he says.

"Thanks" I say, wheeling out of sight. "214, 214, oh here," I mutter. I knock twice before the girl, Claire, opens the door. She looks like she had to sleep in a pit of rats.

"Oh it's you" she says, and shuts the door. I wait six minutes until she comes back, hair neat and wearing her real clothes. "Come in" she says, her voice shaky.

When I walk in it's like seeing a... oh no I hear it 1, 2, 3, 4, 5, 6, 7, 8, 9...79...99, 100. She looks at me and says "Um, not to be rude but... well um..."

I see her sink into the chair beside her bed and I whisper "'Till 100." Her face turns to me so fast I don't know what's coming.

"I've heard that before," she says. I'm startled that she even heard me.

Then I hear a crash. Everything goes dark. I hear a scream. It takes me a moment to realize that scream is coming from me. I collapse on the ground.

The next thing I know, Claire is whispering into my ear, "it's your fault we're like this." I'm in pure shock. *What?* "Now go, I need to rest."

No, it's not my fault, Claire is just a jerk. Then it comes to me, I will never be normal, never, but if I stay like this I won't make friends or go to school. I finally know my decision. It's time to do something about my problems. It's time to face reality.

Chapter 8

The Cure

I go to my parents as quickly as I can. "Mom, Dad, I know what I want. I know what to pick for the 3 choices." I say. They look at me sadly, like they know what I'm going to say, but that they had hoped they would get to pick my fate. "I've decided I want... to have the cure. I know, I know, I might die, but I have to jump. It's like an old saying, *you won't get very far, if you stay where you are*. And I want to go far, I want to *live*. This is my decision, and I have made one, so please tell the doctors to do it immediately."

"Honey..." my mom starts to say.

"No mom, there is nothing to talk about, nothing." I cut her off. She goes quiet.

"Honey we could work this out together, and it's a little fast for a big decision," Dad says.

"No, listen to me, the doctors said it was my decision." I say.

"Alright, we'll tell the doctors immediately," Dad says. I quickly thank them, then I go into the hall to eavesdrop.

"She's our baby, Kaleb," Mom says.

"She wants to do this," Dad says.

"No, we can't let her."

"She is going to tell the doctor herself then."
There is a quiet silence.

"Mom, Dad, I am doing it. You can't change that,
but you can be supportive." They look at me
weirdly.

Perfect timing, Doctor Sam comes in. "Hello Lily,
have you made your decision yet?" He asks.

"Yes! I have chosen the cure." I say.

"Alright, we can do it tomorrow night,
goodnight."

My mother looks petrified, like no doctor in their
right mind would say that so cheery. The truth is I
am super scared, I might die, how would that
feel? Was I good enough to go to heaven? Was it
really my fault? Will I live? All the questions
come at once, the biggest one is: Will I live? I

collapse in my bed, almost instantly I fall asleep. Then the dream comes.

I am *walking* in an empty hall, then I *walk* onto a huge stage, I am in a pretty dress with lilies on it. My hair is wavy and pink. Everyone cheers when I *walk* in. I smile. I start to talk, "When I was younger, I couldn't walk, I was in a wheelchair, then one day a piece of paper arrived, it said that I had three choices:

1. I could get a surgery to remove my legs and get prosthetics

2. I could get a cure that has a 50% chance I could live and 50% chance I could die

3. I could spend the rest of my life in a wheelchair

"I am pretty sure you know what I picked, am I right?" Everyone cheers, then I start to *walk* to the end of the stage. I pull Claire onto the stage with me.

She says, "Thank you."

I wake up with a start. I know what the dream means. Suddenly, a huge boulder I have been carrying falls away and I am left with that light, feather-free feeling once again.

Chapter 9

The True Story

Today is the day! It's gonna happen today! I might be walking out of the hospital tomorrow! Obviously my mom is *not* as excited as I am. When I wake up she is pacing the room like she's on the runway. "Mom?" she turns my way, her face is all puffy and red and it looks like she has been crying all night. What had happened to my mom? I look in the corner and my dad is here! I can't believe it! Usually he would be back in Atlanta by now, but I guess he stuck around! Then I saw a different doctor. I never met her. She was explaining how the operation would go. *Operation? What?! I thought it was a medicine.* I feel a surge of regret.

I slip out of my room to get one last look around the hospital. Then I wheel slowly back to my room.

"Just in time," says a doctor I have never seen before. "My name is Doctor Caroline, you must be Lily." Doctor Caroline says. I nod, now aware of my shaking hands. I grab them and hope mom doesn't notice. "I am going to wheel you to the operation room." She says. I nod. Mom comes up behind me, but Doctor Caroline stops her. "I think it's best if she does this alone," she says.

"She is my baby," Mom says.

"Mom, it's okay." Without waiting for her response, Doctor Caroline and I set off down a hall I have never been in. We finally reach the room. The smell of death is in the air. I shiver. I know you can die from a surgery and it freaks me out. Now I might die too.

She tells me to lie down on the bed and relax, but I can't relax. "I'm going to give you a little shot, okay?" She says.

"Okay" I say, I feel a tiny pinch on my arm, then on the other.

"Now I'm going to count to ten. Imagine you are on an elevator going down into sleep," she says, so I imagine it. "1...2...3...4...5...6...7...8...9...10." A sudden sweep of dizziness washes over me. Then suddenly, I'm in the back of an Uber. Ava and Claire are on either side of me, smiling. We're really excited about being in an Uber without our parents. I'm scared, but they aren't, so I agree. We were going to see <u>Coming to America,</u> of course our parents were going to meet us there though.

"Isn't this fun?" Ava asks. Claire and I nod, we're all wearing matching pink jean jackets with a little dahlia embroidered on it. We wear them everywhere.

"I swear if anyone gets hurt in that..." Claire starts to say.

"No one will get hurt in this car," I say.

She laughs, "I was gonna say movie theater but that works too."

We all laugh, then suddenly a loud horn honks and we laugh again, "Will you kids just shut up?" The driver says, and we burst out into giggles. Then I see a red truck coming right towards us. We're in the wrong lane! I have to say something, but I can't.

Then all I can do is scream to Ava and Claire, "We're in the wrong lane!" then we crash. Ava's door swings open. She falls out as a car drives by. It rolls over her as if she were the road. Then I bonk my head on the door and fall out too. The car rolls over my legs, they get stuck with the wheels. Claire is running away just like the cops told her to. Ava is bleeding and she is going to have to get to a hospital right away.

Then she says, "Keep the jacket...and sing our songs from 'Till 100 to keep our band alive. 'Till 100." Then she stops talking, stops moving, stops breathing. Ava is dead. I am in too much pain. I start to scream and cry. Ava is gone. I see Claire crying too. We go to the hospital right away, but I stay longer than I thought.

Chapter 10

Cured

I wake up. I'm in my hospital bed, safe. My mom is crying with joy. My dad is also crying. I don't know why. "Mom, can you help me get in my wheelchair?" I ask.

"You try." Dad says. I'm so confused, but just then I remember my dream, the surgery, the cure. I try to stand up. I wobble a little, but I do it. Then I try to walk to my wheelchair. I'm doing it, I'm *walking*. I can't believe it. I run and hug my mom and dad. Ava didn't want me to count 'till 100, she wanted me to *sing* 'Till 100, our band. I remember now, everything is picture clear. I ask my parents if I can do something quickly and they say yes. So I run to Claire's room, I knock on the door, Claire answers.

"Claire!" I say. She looks at me and hugs me.

"Lily, I'm so sorry, I was only taking it out on you because I thought it was my fault, I'm the only one who didn't get hurt. Ava died!" We start crying into each other's arms. I tell her the whole story about how it all started at the support group. I tell her how I had the options, then how I had the dream with me walking, then about the surgery and the real story. She holds onto every word I say. When I finally finish, she hugs me again. "Maybe we should sing 'Till 100" Claire says. I nod.

Claire and I are getting ready before the show. We volunteered to sing a song we made for the hospital before we leave. We put on our pink jean jackets with the dahlia on it (surprisingly it still fits). "It's showtime." We walk on stage (or what's close to a stage).

"Hello everyone," Claire says.

"We are going to be singing *Forget The Past*, a song we made with our band "Till 100," I say. "We hope you like it."

Forget The Past

"I've been catching every word we say
and I know we stay longer
but now we're stronger
and so much has happened
and so much is coming this way
and this is what you wanted, uhh ohh, yeah
we can take you home
Every second we spend
Every word that we lend
yeah this is who we are

and we've gotten so far
but we are so much stronger
we are so much better
and I'd like to thank this world
cause without this we're nothing
I know you would rather be over there
you were granted and enchanted
you always haunted
So I think we were free
and I think that we see
that this was meant to be
So forget, forget the past
we know the truth in our value
So forget, forget the past
we know we've got it in our heart
we won't fall apart
we got you all wrong
we're saying it in this song
don't worry it's not long."

Author's Note

I originally wrote this story for my sister, Karuna. She loves to read books about kids with disabilities. I created the character, Lily, because she has an interesting story. The story is no love story you would see in a movie. This is a love story about teaching Lily to love herself.

Acknowledgements

I would like to thank my mom, Megan Schiller, for helping me make this story come alive. Thank you to my dad, Aaron Schiller, for giving me the assignment to write a book outline during early Covid homeschooling. Thanks to my sister, Karuna Schiller, for giving me the inspiration to write this story and to my dog, Maisy for just being you. To my third grade teacher, Jeffry Krieger, thank you for encouraging me to finish my stories. Thank you to my Nana (Deborah) for always asking about my writing. And thanks to Micah, Amari, Satya, Noah, Saba (Don), G-Bob, Grandma (Joan), Grandpa (Mike), Caity, and Jake for reading an early draft and being so supportive.

About The Author

Ora Schiller has always loved to read and write. Reading stories was a getaway from the real world, then she found out she could create any world just by typing out a story plot. Ora spends a lot of time writing, but she also does a whole lot more. She likes to run around with friends in the neighborhood, do fun art projects, sing, act, dance, and do gymnastics. She lives in Northern California with her mom, dad, sister, and dog, Maisy. Ora is 9 years old. This is her first book.

Made in the USA
Las Vegas, NV
24 April 2021